I0557174

Broken In Broad Daylight

Marquessa Prater

Broken In Broad Daylight

Broken In Broad Daylight

DEDICATION

"I would like to dedicate this book to my favorite girl in Heaven, "My Grandmother Georgia W. Piedro A.K.A. Grama. "If it wasn't for your encouragement, prayers, and love growing up, I don't think I would have made it this far to write this book. "I know you are smiling down from heaven. "We did it. I thank you & always love you. ~ Quessa

Broken In Broad Daylight

CONTENTS

ACKNOWLEDGMENTS

'I would like to take the time out to give thanks to God; you witness obstacles I face that no one will ever know. "It was you that kept me and wanted me to finish this race to share my talent with the world, and I can't thank you enough. To Author, V.Brown, thank you for encouraging and motivating me to write my book over the years continue to shine, queen. My Mother, Courtney P. Wright, for seeing my vision giving advice, and encouraging me along the way I love you. My Father, Henry Williams, and Bonus Father, Andre Wright, thank you both for giving me fatherly advice that I can count on when I needed love you both. To all My Siblings, Nephews, Nieces (1Deceased), Grandparents (3Deceased), Work Mothers, Adopted God Fathers (R.I.P.), Aunties, Uncles, Cousins, Goddaughter, Families in Christ, Close Friends and Deceased Close Friends. "I love each and one of you thank you for all the love, prayers and support over the years. To Olop_pics, Larry The Designer, Lafattythemua and The Legendary Way "Thank you all for listening to my vision and bringing it to life everyone did a phenomenal job. "Thank you to everyone who purchase my book in person or online I want to thank you in advance. Last but certainly not least, The Author of Broken In Broad Daylight "Marquessa Prater I'm so proud of myself it was a lot of rest stops, but I kept the faith and kept my trust in God and finishedthisrace."

Chapter One
"THE OAKWOOD'S"

The all-black 2021 Jeep Wrangler on gold 26's rims is flying by playing "The Boss by Rick Ross on D-Block. "The dope boys immediately stop with their dice game, card games drug sell, smoking and drinking their bottles of Hennessey. Aye, that's The Oakwood's. "I heard about them they from Liberty City heard the cat name Dollar the number 1 Drug Dealer down there. Lonnie replied. "Oh Yeah, " Ounce responded, all attention focus on D-Block as the 2021 Jeep Wrangler, 10 Oversize Mercedes Benz U-Haul's Trucks, and five furniture trucks from every high-end furniture store you can imagine from Lexington, Coaster, Hooker, Bernhard, Stanley Furniture Trucks, all zoom by approaching their new home on 63rd and Curtis. Damn! "I have never seen anything like this on the block neighbors rushing off their porch, kids eyes feel with exciting racing their bikes betting each other hot fries, frozen cups, and hot sausages as they ride their bikes following The Oakwood's and all the other trucks drivers to The Oakwood's new home. "I bet that's A Rapper NO! Man, that's A Movie Star, NO! That's The President.

Meanwhile, you got Monica, the Biggest Groupie on D-Block, hopping off her porch with a crop top, bonnet, house shoes, and shorts that look like underwear. "Move out the way kids coming threw I got things to see and people to meet. "God, please let this be my new baby father," praying as she looks up to the sky. Monica, Monica as Courtney shout down the sidewalk, "I'll be back girl Monica replied. The Oakwood's and truck drivers approach their new home on D-Block to open their privacy gate on command. All vehicles enter the gate and immediately shut after. Kids on D-Block and Monica didn't make it to the gate on time before it was shut, leaving everyone full of disappointment. All the kids turned around and went back home. Monica is trying to jump over the wall as the security gate responds; you have 2 seconds to leave off the premises. "Monica took off running back towards her home as she made it back she saw Courtney on her Porch out of breath girl I couldn't jump over the wall. " Girl you really need some help you literally ran over those kids you are so money hungry you don't know anything about those people. That's the point once I show the owner a good time my pockets will go ching, ching "Laughing" you know what I mean? No! I don't bye Monica! " As the Movers stared, unloading trucks. Diamond, Tesla, and Mercedes went rushing into their new home. Oh my goodness, this is an absolutely beautiful Diamond, respond in tears. Mercedes and Tesla rush upstairs, claiming rooms. "Mama come see upstairs as Mercedes and Tesla shouted downstairs. I'm coming; girls Dollar walk in after talking with the loaders and making phone calls with his connect in MIA. "Yes, Sir! Yes Sir, as Dollar smiling from ear to ear. " Looking up to the bay windows, world-class lighting crystal chandelier, glancing overlooking The build in aquarium making his way over to the kitchen with all black and gold granite countertops with a gold backslash and gold & black marble floors, black cabinets with gold trimming and 24 karats gold build-in appliances. Man, what hustler, you know got a deck out mansion that takes up two blocks from 63rd to 65th in the hood "We have a four-car garage both of my daughters drive cars after their names, we own five cars ,a private jet and four jet skis. "We have robot housekeeper, elevator, indoor & outdoor pool. Signs directing you were The Gym, Game Room, Movie Theater and His & Her Beauty Bar. "Man, this $731,000 home PAID IN FULL was well worth it for my three lovely ladies. If anything happens to me, I know they'll be straight. Dollar shouted, "Diamond, Mercedes & Tesla, come downstairs, come tell me what you think about our new home. Everyone came rushing downstairs, embracing Dollar with hugs and kisses. "Baby, you out did yourself Diamond, kissing Dollar over and over again. Her tears were dropping over Dollar face. Baby, don't cry. I told you I got yall forever; everything is paid for. Dollar turns from after kissing Diamond to pulling Mercedes and Tesla together on each of his arms and turning towards the couch; let's sit, "Daddy wants to talk with the both of you. Look, Daddy loves both of you very much. Both of you are to the age to know the truth about where daddy works. "I'm a big-time drug dealer daddy's name is well known. Back in the day daddy used to be in this gang called Choppers. Daddy was raising himself at an early age after your Grandmother Mama P passed the streets was all I know. Growing up, it was rough for me to find jobs without graduating, but I had to find fast money after finding out your mother was pregnant with Cedes. I wanted to make sure I could provide everything for your Mother, so she wouldn't have to work nor need anything while finishing school. You both deserve to hear the truth from me. If anyone ever questions you, walk away and call me immediately. Do you both understand me? "Yes, daddy, we do. I put everything in both of your names. I want you both to be better than me, and so far, you both are I'm very proud of the mature, respectful young ladies you are. Tesla continue to focus on graduating daddy, waiting for his other baby to walk across that stage. Mercedes, I'm very proud of you for enrolling into college. "Thank you, daddy." I want both of you to be better than me. I have two Trust Funds at Morris Bank with $100,000 in both accounts for the both of you. "The both of you are not to touch the money until you complete high school and college. Your Mother, know where all the flies are for our family lawyer, keys and money at. Cedes, always watch out for your baby sister, and Diamond, always watch out for the girls. We are a team. Who are we? The Oakwood's, who are we? The Oakwood's, who are we? The Oakwood's. Better believe it! I love all three of my lovely ladies. "Welcome to our new home. "Now go shower up and get dress. We are celebrating I'm about to call the pilot to get ready for takeoff; we are flying to Beverly Hills to Eat at The Penthouse. "I'm a Boss, and we do **BOSS SHIT!**

Chapter Two
"Senior Year"

Broken In Broad Daylight

"Alarm going off, I can smell the aroma of the bacon and eggs that the robot prepares. " Mama shouting Tesla and Mercedes, come down and eat breakfast. Oh, Mercedes, bring down your paperwork for enrollment for college. "Yes, ma'am both replied. Good morning Mama, as Mercedes and Tesla enter the dining room. Good morning; my baby's Diamond walk to both of them, embracing with a kiss on the cheek. "Your father and I are so proud of both of you. I can't believe I now have an adult child, and my baby is almost an adult in another year. Tears were running down mama's face. I don't care how old both of you get. Remember, this always home. Tesla, are you excited on your first day of your senior year? Yes, Ma'am, just wait until you see my new drip girl, please! Cedes replied (Laughing) what are you wearing? Diamond and Mercedes ask my Versace Dress, Versace Headband, and Versace Heels almost forget my Maison Francis Fragrance Kurkdjan. "Got to smell like money when I walk through. You are an Oakwood for sure sound just like your daddy, "Mama replied. "Good morning, my lovely ladies. Good morning, baby, we just talk you up. What I did? Your baby girl sound just like you talking about what she is wearing to school. Diamond sips her coffee and shakes her head. I want you to enjoy your last year in high school but focus on graduating at the same time. As hard it may seem, I have to face the fact you are not a baby anymore. "This is the year I will be buying homecoming and prom dresses, cap and gown, grad night tickets, and you talking about dating. " Oh lord, I'm not ready; please don't grow up to fast, Tesla. "I'm not daddy" Tesla came around the table to hug her and kiss her daddy. I promise to make you and mama proud, daddy. Let me go get dress, so I won't be late for my first day. Okay, baby. Tesla rush upstairs quickly turns on the shower; the steam from the shower fog up the mirrors in Tesla bathroom. She wrote, "Da Baddest Senior at Roosevelt High C/O 2021. "Alexa play Lil Boosie "Wipe Me Down. "I get downstairs there go daddy and mama done hired a Photographer. Girl, you look good sis; thank you, sis, as she kisses Cedes on the cheek. Mama crying like this her last time seeing me and daddy look at my baby girl. The Photographer didn't even have to direct me on how to pose. I did what I had to do. I stopped and told The Photographer I wanted my favorite people in a photo with me. "He smiles" Daddy, Mama, and Cedes come take a photo with me; they immediately hope in, and it was picture perfect. Okay, everyone, I have to go; this was a great surprise, thank you. I love everyone so much. Have a good first day baby, knock them, dead sis. I turned on my car and put it in the direction in the GPS to Roosevelt High, and played "Da Baddest Bitch" by Trina. As my car drives down the road, I'm snapping photos posting on all my social media platforms. I pull up to school, all eyes on me. I had the hottest car at Roosevelt High. I see the faculties whispering and pointing as I got out of the car." I wave, so they will know I see them whispering about me. Ms. Smith almost dropped her coffee. I walk to my homeroom # 202. As I walk into the room, Good morning, my name is Mr. Troy. "I'm your Homeroom Teacher, and you are. "Good morning, my name is Tesla Oakwood. It's a pleasure to meet you. "Here is your new schedule. Let me know if you need anything. "Feel free to sit anywhere" Okay, thank you. Tesla over here, Destiney, I save you a seat. Yes, Cha-Cha and Destiny come through. You both look good. Girl, you look good too. Destiny snapped a picture of us and posted us on her IG. Notifications instantly came threw we had over 300 likes in 15mins. Aye, that's them, "look like the boys in room 202 spotted us on IG. "Bell ring Cha-Cha, Destiny, and I started giggling and laughing, walking out the door. We were walking down the hallway. Damn! They all fine boys respond, and girls turning up their nose and rolling their eyes, and there go Destiney shooting a bird and me and Cha-Cha just laughing. Destiny is the wild one, the one that doesn't give a care what comes out of her mouth about her money and protects her family and friends by any means. Chasity A.K.A Cha-Cha is very quiet, smart, and a teenage mother to an eight-month old daughter named Star, then it's me mature, caring, spoil, and have trust issues when it comes to friends. "When I see your loyalty, I'm your friend forever. Intercom comes on as I reach my first period class. Good Morning! Lions at Roosevelt High. My name is Mr. Ross. I'm your Principal. "I'm happy to share this awarding year with my faculties, students, parents, and visitors. "Please show respect to your peers and our staff; everyone has a good first day. Your principal Mr. Ross "So much for respect I'm feeling out of place you ever went to a cookout or a party and felt overdress. Well, that was me. The females look like they roll out of bed. "Still have on their pajamas bonnets and house shoes. The guys smell like musk and old spice pants below their waist, so unattractive. Like I know everyone is not fortunate enough like me. Hell, I would have accept a Great Value Outfit from Walmart then this. "My Versace looks like a knockoff. " This is a hot mess. Meanwhile my first period Math Teacher Ms. Hart does roll call, she has been on (B) names for over 2 minutes seems like. All I could think about is graduation, praying she is not the person that calls names to receive my diploma. She is talking so slow if I was deaf, I could hear it. I'm about to put my phone in my book and play like I'm reading and look what they got new in on Chanel Website. I know I won't miss anything. I'm learning something today multitasking. "Oh, those shoes are nice $2,500, not bad at all. I got to have them. Checkout Complete. "Thank you, Ms. Oakwood. Your payment was accepted, expect your order to arrive in 24hrs. "Today is starting out great. Ms. Oakwood, Ms. Oakwood, Ms. Oakwood. "Ms. Hart is calling me. Can you tell the class about yourself? "My apologies, Ms. Hart. I was reading a scripture. Good morning everyone, my name is Tesla Oakwood. I just move from Miami, in the biggest house on 63rd, Got money, I drive a Tesla, Family owns a Private Jet, Trying to graduate, and don't need any new friends. I have two Best Friend's Destiney and Cha-Cha. "A pleasure to meet everyone, "bow to the class" and sat down. What an intro Ms. Hart replied, Welcome! Bell ring "good I only got to walk four doors down. "I'm happy Destiny and I have 2nd-period History together. Destiny was coming to Mr. Donell History Class with a straight unit on her face. "Now, why would Roosevelt High do that to me? What happened? My 1st period was P.E. "I'm mad as hell it was so hot got us running the track and shit! If I knew that shit! I would have been late. "Girl, look at my damn lace and my makeup is dripping. Mr. Ross needs to refund me back my $1,000. I'm putting P.E right in these damn history books..." I bet tomorrow is going to have a new 1st-period class. I'm about to ask for a slip to the principal office now. Excuse Mr. Donell as Destiny shouted as she paces to Mr. Donell Desk with her hand on her hip with a sassy attitude. "I need to be excused to go to the Principal's Office. Is there something wrong that I can help with? "Yeah, do you have $1000 to fix my lace? "I'm afraid I don't, and you are? Destiny Bradshaw as Mr. Donell write Destiny a slip to the Principal's Office. "I hope everything works out, Ms. Bradshaw. "Oh, it will as he gets up out of his seat, walking around his desk, walking Destiny to the door. See you later Tesla. "Attention all on me now. Mr.Donell walks over with his arm extend release as he greeted me and you are? Good morning Tesla Oakwood. "I see we are going to have a little trouble? "No, Sir? She's just upset about her hair and makeup and wants the Principal to change her schedule from P.E. "I see may it work in her favor, and that they change her schedule." Good Morning, everyone. My name is Mr. Donell. Welcome to 2nd period History.

Chapter Three
"Drive Down D-Block"

"Damn, it's hotter than a chilly pepper out here; before I head home, I need to hit up Smacks on D-Block for a Slurpee, Reese's, and some Boil Peanuts. " I'm about to let all the windows down and let back my sunroof and blast the air. "Traffic moving so slow the city bus stop every 2 seconds at another bus stop. I don't know why they got these bus stops so close together. "Great, another red light beep, beep, beep the Range Rover, to the left of me, honking the horn. I can see him bout to make love to the steering wheel, trying to get my attention. I'm paying him no mine. He rolls down the windows, so you don't hear me blowing at you? Damn, why you got to look so mean? "He better be lucky this light turn green. He was about to get a piece of my mind. As I turn on D-Block really reminds me of back home. Girls walking down the street with carts they stole from the grocery store, crack heads, kids running outside with no shoes, thugs posted up or playing a dice game, and someone running to the bus stop, with the driver pulling off soon as they reach the bus stop. Let me roll up my windows and close this sunroof and grab my purse "This is not the time to test my luck. "I press the alarm going into the store. "I walk into Smacks; the Arab Store Owner greeted me with Hello! Hello, how are you beautiful? I'm fine! That you are my name is Mahan I have never seen you in here before. Hello, my name is Tesla. I just move here; welcome, let me know if you need anything. Okay, I will thank you. You're quite welcome as he leans on the counter with his head bent to the side smiling as I walk to the back to make my Slurpee and Boil Peanuts. Oh, I almost forgot, let me grab My Reese's. As I arrive back at the counter, placing my items on the countertop as Mahan started to bag up my items, the door open. "Aye, Mahan, I got it. I'll cover this beautiful lady tab. I can pay for my stuff as I still face the counter. "I never said you couldn't, but a thank you would be nice. THANK YOU! Damn, it's like that. Why do you got to be so rude? "You're beautiful, but you got a stuck-up attitude let me change that. My name is Rayquan, and you are? Tesla turns as she was about to give her name but was so amazed by Rayquan's appearance. He was 6' foot, Dark Chocolate skin complexion his lips, smile, well groom had an all-white Burberry Collar Shirt, Starch Khaki Shorts, and Burberry Sneakers and his aroma from his cologne I can smell that he had on Tom Ford (F^^king Fabulous). "I apologize. My name is Tesla. It's nice to meet you. "I have never seen you around. Are you new in town? Yes, I just move from Miami. Oh, word, welcome to Tampa. What's your number?

"His homeboy Ounce walks back in the store, Mahan lets me get two Backwoods aye Quan, let's go stop sweating that stuck-up bitch. "Man, who are you calling a bitch? You stuck-up bitch you want a nigga to beg you and shit. Hoes these days. Aye, chill Ounce, this is a female show some respect. Fuck that; I would have left that hoe. Aye, I will be outside rolling up. Man, I apologize for my homeboy. This why I don't give niggas time of the day now. "I hope you're not like him." No, I'm not. I was raised differently. My Big Mama, didn't play that. "Well, good. " Let me walk you to your car. Make sure you get there safely. "Man, it's right there, so what's your number? I see you don't give up "My number is (305)071-3118. Ok, I will be calling you soon. Drive safe, beautiful. Rayquan walking from the car, Are you ready? Rayquan said to Ounce been ready. Ounce, I don't know why you are sweating these hoes. "You need to show some respect to females; that shit wasn't cool Ounce. "I arrive back home; no one is home. I'm about to watch a movie in the theater and eat my snacks. I lean back in the recliner as the film was about to start. I receive an incoming face time notification. "Who number is this? I hesitate if I should accept the call or not. "I accept the call Hello Beautiful! " It was Rayquan. I hope I didn't disturb you. Is this a good time to talk?

Chapter Four
"House Divided Leaving Brokenhearted "

4:00 AM hear loud stomps coming up the stairs. "This my shit, I'm the king of this bitch. Daddy is so intoxicated. Screaming mama's name. Diamond, where your ass at? Let's dance Diamond, where you at baby? Daddy burg in their room. Oh, so you are ignoring me wake your ass up. "You can hear mama's footsteps racing to the door to close it before Cedes, and I heard the loud disturbances, but it was too late. Cedes and I was already in the hallway. Go back to sleep girls, I love you both. Before mama, could shut the door, their go, daddy, Tesla, Cedes, give daddy some love. Go back to sleep, my baby's. Oh, so you are trying to lock the door; why I'm talking to our children? Baby, you are intoxicated. "The girls don't need to see you like this. Fuck you bitch. That's why I should have married someone else, you selfish bitch. Go back to sleep, girls. I can see that mama was pissed at daddy's actions. As the door close. Daddy started fighting mama BOOM (repeated) all you hear at the door. Cedes and I was trying to open the door. Daddy stop open the door, you hurting mama No, this bitch is trying me. I'm going to give your mama what she deserves. I can hear mama saying, "I rebuke you evil spirit from the pits of hell in the mighty name of Jesus. For God has set me free. "I never heard mama talk spiritually before. Daddy, please answer the door. Meanwhile, Cedes is calling 911. Daddy finally

Broken In Broad Daylight

opens the door. I instantly ran to mama, crying in her blood as she started to get up. I can't believe I have taken your mess for over 18yrs from the cheating, a miscarriage, and disrespect I had enough. The devil is a liar. My baby's will not see their mother being abuse. "I love you Dollar but no longer in love with you. " So you leaving me Diamond? Mama went over to daddy; no, you are. Cedes had let the police in the house. The officers give daddy his rights and ask him to put his hands behind his back as they put the handcuffs on him and walk daddy downstairs. Daddy stopped and said, "Can I please have a second with my girls? The officers agree to let daddy talk to us. Cedes and Tesla "I want the both of you to know daddy love the both of you very much. I'm sorry that I hurt both of you and Diamond. Please! Don't hate your daddy; just know daddy loves the both of you so much. He kisses Cedes and me on the forehead. Mama was standing on the edge of the stairs, full of emotions. "I love you, Diamond. I'm so sorry I put my hands on you and disrespect you in front of our children. Mama looks at daddy and turns and walks back upstairs. Okay, Mr. Oakwood, we must go now. Thank you, officers, for letting me talk to my girls. As daddy got in the police car. He looks at Cedes and I as tears ran down his face. Cedes and I put our arms around each other and hold each other tight while tears continue to race down our faces. We went upstairs to check on mama; as we came into our parents' room, mama was reading scriptures from the bible. Come here, girls, get in bed with me. Cedes went on one side; I went on the other. Never let any man sit and hit you or disrespect you. "I can't believe for over 18yrs I have put up with this from your father. " I apologize to the both of you for what took place tonight. "Trust me; it was the last time mama kiss the both of us. The remainder of the night Cedes, and I just stayed and slept with mama. "I had so many questions running in my head and pain in my heart tonight. "I look at daddy like my hero, my protector, never thought that daddy and mama would split up in a million years. I got back up that morning at 10:00 AM. Mama and Cedes were still sleeping. I kissed mama and went back to my room. I turn on the shower and just let the water hit my face. As the water connected with my tears, I'm so hurt by this. I got out of the shower, dried off, put on some joggers and a tank top, and laid across my bed and listen to music. I receive a morning text from Rayquan. It read:

Rayquan: Good morning, beautiful "I hope you slept good last night.
Tesla: Good morning, I didn't feeling very emotional
Rayquan: I'm here for you if you want to talk about it
Tesla: "I might just take you on that offer.
Rayquan: Let's meet at Garden Park "I will pin the location.
Tesla: I will be there in 20mins
Rayquan: Ok, I'm on the way

"I went to mama room to let her know I was leaving to go to the park. Good morning mama, "Good morning, baby how are you? About to go to park to clear my head. Do you want Cedes and I to go with you? No, I just want this time alone. Okay, baby, be careful. "I will" I arrive at Garden Park Rayquan was already at the park sitting on the hood of his car looking at the water view. "As I pull up, Rayquan noticed me and immediately jumped off his car to come and greet me. " He didn't say anything but embrace me with open arms. We hug for over 30seconds the connection I could tell Rayquan been through this or been broken before. Once we got done hugging each other, he stared at me and said, it will be Ok. He grabs my hands and began to walk close to the water. There was this log you can sit on. We sat there for hours just talking about life; Rayquan started, telling me that he lost both of his parents when he was 15yrs old. They were involved in a car accident. A truck driver fell asleep at the wheel. He then moves to stay with his Grandmother, Hattie Mae, and she passed away when he was 16yrs old. "Leaving him with no one to turn to but the streets and dropping out of school at an early age. " I felt terrible about what I heard from Rayquan. I'm so blessed that I have both of my parents and sister. "I'm not sure if I could live without them. " We started walking, talking about our favorite movies, songs, foods, scriptures from the bible, what we wanted to become, and places where we want to visit throwing rocks in the water. There was this hill Rayquan said the last one there is a rotten egg. On you, marc, get set go. Guess who was the rotten egg? Me, of course. "I like that Rayquan had a great sense of humor knew how to have fun. " I felt so much better. I turn to Rayquan and thank him for taking the time out to meet me. "He kisses me on the forehead like daddy does and said anytime. " I knew right there he was the person I wanted to be with. "All these years, I had my guard up and never gave any guy the time of day. Today was the day I realize all boys are not the same and don't be so quick to judge. "I arrive home Mama, and Cedes, were out by the pool. " Hey, baby, are you feeling better? Yes, ma'am, I am. How are you? I'm good. I have my baby's, and that's all that matters to me. Mama had the Robot Chef make us Strawberry Frozen Daiquiris and Cuban Sandwiches. I went upstairs to change in my swimsuit. As I was coming back downstairs, I can see mama threw the glass door up dancing by the pool. I instantly smile; it felt good to see everyone having a good time. Tesla; let me show you and Cedes my moves how I got your daddy. "Mama was doing splits, and all". "We laugh, dance ate, talk, and listen to music. "Only person missing was daddy."

Chapter Five

"Girls Just Want To Spend Funds "

The next day Mama, Cedes, and I went to Legends Mall. It was high in mall in Tampa where all ballers, celebrities go has nothing but the best high in stores and five-star restaurants. Not your average mall, it had a golf course, derby, a bank, casino, and a monorail to travel to the airport. Mama wanted to go to Neiman Marcus, and Cedes wanted to go into Chanel, and of course, I was in heaven; this is therapy for me. "Welcome to Neiman Marcus. Are you shopping for anything particular today? No, we are just browsing but thank you, mama respond. We pick up shoes after shoes. The salesman oh, these are $750, and those are $940. Very expensive ma'am, I'm pretty aware of the price. Oh, I didn't mean to offend you, ma'am, "oh, you didn't I will take both in size 10 in every color. The salesman had to get two other employees to assist him. Mama sat and tried on every color just to piss the salesman off and only got the red ones. So ma'am, you are not getting all the shoes we carry out? No all 29 pairs of shoes can go back for the 29mins you pissed me off and the one pair I'll take for the minute I had alone out the 30 minutes. "Next time, don't be so quick to judge people off the color of their skin; not all white are rich, and all black are not poor, but if I wanted all 30 pairs of shoes, I could. "I'll save that for next time for a salesman that would appreciate their customers and not be so judgmental. "My apologies, ma'am; your total and is $799.99. Mama gave him $800.00 and told him to keep the change and grab her receipt and bag. Cedes and I thought that was so hilarious. We continue to walk around the mall. Cedes got her a Chanel Dress and Chanel Headband. "I got another pair of Chanel Shades and a pair of Chanel Sandals. " As we walk out the store, mama wanted to pause on shopping and go get a bite to eat. At Ruth's Chris, she had a taste for a Tomahawk Rib Eye Steak, Creamed Spinach, and Mash Potatoes.

Cedes: "Mama, that sound's good. I can taste their Stuffed Chicken Breast now Mmmmm

Tesla: Guess I have Salmon Filet and Caesar salad

Ruth's Chris Host: "Good Afternoon welcome to Ruth's Chris. "How many are in your party? "

Mama: there will be 3 for "Oakwood's

Ruth's Chris Host:" there will be a 10min wait; feel free to have a seat in our lobby. Your waiter will be with you momentarily.

Waiter: Party of 3 for Oakwood's "The Waiter showed us to our seats Good afternoon my name is Donald "I will be your Waiter for today "could I start you out with a drink and appetizers?

Mama: I will have a Pomegranate Martini & Calamari for an appetizer

Cedes: I will have a Coke and Water

Tesla: I will have a Sprite

Waiter: "I will give you some time to look over the menu. I will be back with your beverages and appetizers shortly.

Mama: ok, thank you

As the waiter left our table, we started looking over the menu. We already knew what we wanted, but we played it off. We didn't want to look so greedy. Hey, mama, when the Waiter comes back to take our orders. Could you order me a Salmon Filet, Baked Potatoes, and Caesar Salad? "I have to go to the restroom' Mama: ok baby, I will let him know." I excuse myself from the table; after coming out of the restroom, I bump into a guy in the hallway. Excuse me, I apologize

Ounce: Aye, don't I know you?

Tesla: "You were the disrespectful friend that was at Smacks with Rayquan the other day, right?

Ounce: Yeah, that's me. I apologize; let's start over. : "My name is Ounce

Tesla: My name is not interested.

Ounce: "You a Boujee Ass Bitch, I don't know why I even talk to you.
Tesla: "I don't know why you did either.

Ounce: "I can't wait to tell Rayquan who I saw. Today:

Tesla: "You don't have to; he is calling me now. "Here the phone."

Ounce: F^^K You

Tesla: "You wish you could; your time is up; I gave you enough role-play today. " Around of applause for the scene "Lil Boy."

"I had missed Rayquan's first call, but he called right back.

Broken In Broad Daylight

Rayquan: Hello Beautiful, how is your day going?

Tesla: It was going well until   I met your disrespectful friend. "Just now in Ruth's Chris

Rayquan: Who Ounce?

Tesla: As I was walking out of the restroom, I bump into him "he notice who I was. "He was trying to run game, and I didn't give him the time of day; now, I'm this Boujee Bitch and all that other mess. "Forget him; he doesn't deserve to be in our conversation. How are you doing today?

Rayquan: Good, now I'm talking to you.

Tesla: 'I'm happy to hear that'" Can we talk later? "I need to get back to the table. I know my family is wondering what is taking me so long.

Rayquan: ok, beautiful, and I will talk to Ounce; he won't be disrespecting you anymore.

Tesla: thank you. "I will talk to you later (Called Ended)

"Is everything ok, baby? " Yes, ma'am, it's just some immature people, you know. Trust me, baby I know. The Waiter came out with our food everything looks delicious. "Mama always has us to pray before we eat as we were eating, I wanted to ask mama how she feels about me dating.

Tesla: Mama, Can I ask you a question?

Mama: sure, baby!

Tesla: How do you feel about me dating?

Mama: Well, I'm never ready, but you are to the age where you will start dating, fall in love, sexual active and might have your heartbroken. "A Mother's Prayer is that you never fall in my footsteps be better than me. " I know I can't choose who you will date and love. "Just remember you are the table, and he better come with it when he is dating you. "Do you have someone you crushing on?

Tesla: "Yes ma'am, it's this guy name Rayquan. I met him at Smacks the other day coming from school; he makes me laugh, respectful, handsome and shows me attention and definitely talk about God; it feels like I knew him for a long time

Cedes: Sis, I know that look; that's how I felt about Jahiem and no one I have met yet since he died. "Makes me feel the way he did."

Mama: Cedes, give it some time Jahiem is truly missed it took some time for me to accept him because you were at the age when I got pregnant with you. I was afraid you would fall into my footsteps, and you indeed prove me wrong. "I had to learn to trust and accept I can't choose your man for you. " I'm very proud of the both of you. Cedes and Tesla. "I want you both to always come to me if you need anything. "You both are my seeds, and I will never turn on you.

Cedes: Awww, I love you so much mama,

Tesla: I love you too mama; always "thank you for that advice and a great time today.

Mama: anything for my girls

Waiter: How was everything?

Oakwood's: Great!

Waiter: Would anyone like dessert?

Oakwood's: No, thank you

After lunch, we headed to do a little more shopping. After leaving the mall, mama turn on her tunes. Cedes was completing her essay that's due tomorrow, and I'm just was in the back seat texting Rayquan. "He wants to take me out Friday and show me around Tampa. I hesitated to reply back to the text because I would hate to let him down with a NO! I have to find a way to ask mama. This might be the perfect time while she is driving and not looking at me and listening to music. "Hoping she says yes after the talk we just had a Ruth's Chris. Here it goes "I'm just going to ask NOW!

Tesla: Mama, you recall when you said Cedes, and I can ask you anything

Mama: "Yes, baby, what is it?

Tesla: Oh No, mama turning down the music looking at me in the rearview mirror. "God, you didn't work in my favor with this one, but "Here it goes," Rayquan would like to take me out Friday after school and show me around Tampa. " Can I go? "I'm sweating like hell in the back seat of mama's response.

Mama: "Yes, I will let you go, but you have to be home by 12:00 AM

Tesla: I unbuckle my seatbelt so fast and hug mama from the back of the seat. "Thank you, mama, you're the best. One more thing!

Mama: What is it, Tesla?

Tesla: can I make a quick trip on the jet to Beverly Hills with Cha-Cha and Destiny after school? I promise to be back before 11:00 P.M.?

Mama: Tesla, you're pushing it now. I'm going to let you go the minute I see you're not focusing on your schoolwork; everything will be cut off. Do I make myself clear?

Tesla: Yes, ma'am, I won't disappoint you

"I felt so relieved that mama said yes. I text Rayquan back so fast and let him know I can go out with him Friday,

Chapter 6
"GIRL TALK & QUICK FLIGHT"

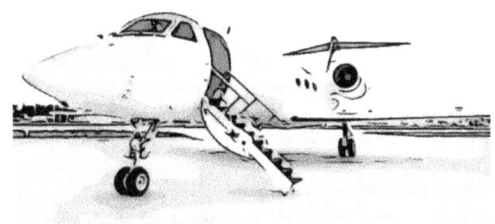

"Soon as we got home, I went home and shower and was anxious to tell Cha-Cha and Destiny the news. "Let me call them up.

Tesla: "what's up, Cha-Cha?

Cha-Cha: Nothing girl feeding Star & then bathe her and get her ready for bed. What's up with you?

Tesla: Kiss ti-ti stank for me "Girl guess what? " No, hold the line, let me call Destiney on 3way. "So I can tell you both the news at the same time. " What's up, Destiny? What are you up to? "Oh and Cha-Cha and Star on the line, btw

Cha-Cha: What's up, Destiny?

Destiny: Hey yall and hey ti-ti baby, I love you. I'm just finding my outfit for my stage set for Saturday Night at Tasty's. "What's tea?

Tesla: Girl, how you are stripping at Tasty's and only 18yrs old?

Destiny: I got connections nobody gave me shit! "I got to provide for Big Mama and Lil Zack. "That McDonald's job didn't cut it. "They cut off Big Mama food stamps, lights twice, and Lil Zack need school clothes, Big Mama "Only makes $735 on Social Security that only covers rent. Ever since my mom passed away." I had to make sure I pull my weight and take care of Big Mama and Lil Zack. "Nobody is not handing me shit!

Cha-Cha: "I know that's right! Destiny. "I don't care how many quick weaves I got to do or men I have to use. "I got to do what I got to do to make sure Star and I will eat and live comfortably.

Tesla: Ok, I didn't mean to offend anyone. I do have it a little better than others. "Just know I'm always here for the both of you if anyone ever needs me.

Cha-Cha: "It's ok girl I didn't take it to heart

Destiny: "I didn't either best friend; now, what's the tea?

Tesla: I want yall to fly to Beverly Hills with me tomorrow after school just for a couple of hours.

Cha-Cha: Girl, what say no more? I'm down; let me pay one of my Lil Cousins to watch Star for me. "I love my baby but need this break."

Destiny: Hell Yeah! "I will go; what made you want to fly to Beverly Hills?

Tesla: " It's been so much going on; daddy lock up for hitting mama, but mama is ok the family feels so divided since he got arrest. " I need this time with my girls and find something to wear to go on a date with my new boo.

Destiny: Girl, what new boo, not you? Why are you just telling us about him?

Cha-Cha: Yes, why?

Tesla: I just had to make sure he is the one and trust he is. "He has been there to lift my sprints ever since all this happened in my household. Of course, daddy doesn't know about him, but mama and Cedes do just haven't met him yet.

Destiny: Girl, I'm so happy for you

Cha-Cha: Me too. I'm so ready to hear more about him.

Tesla: "Get your rest, ladies; got a long day tomorrow."

(Called Ended)

"As we prepare to take the flight, Destiny and Cha-Cha was so hype. "Destiny, run to the jet girl, take my picture. "This Jet is so freaking nice Tesla. One more Tesla, "Make sure you get my shoes come on Cha-Cha get in this once in a life time. "We love you Tesla" The flight attendant ask if we wanted anything off the menu. Cha-Cha quickly responded with a NO! "I know this stuff is too high. " I told her to get what she wants; everything is FREE; we own it. "In that case, may I have Shrimp, Fries, Oreo Cheesecake, and Coke for my drink?

Destiny: I will take a Hamburger with No! Mayo, Onion Rings, and Sprite to drink? "Tesla, what are you going to eat?

Tesla: "I will have Ten Wings all flats and Sweet Tea

Destiny: Thank you, girl, for this trip "when we get to Beverly Hills, I'm going to look for something for my stage set. " I know no one will have my drip. Cha-Cha: "Man Tesla this jet is so lovely. "I'm glad God blessed me with a friend like you. "How can I repay you?

Tesla: "You already did by showing me what a true friend is.

Destiny: "Excuse me, ma'am, would you mind taking our picture?

Flight Attendant Tracy: Certainly

Tesla: Destiny came over behind Cha-Cha, and I and stood in the middle and lean in on us as the Flight Attendant Tracy took our picture.123 Best Friends Forever. "Buckle up, ladies Beverly Hills, here we come. "We arrive at Beverly Hills. This was Cha-Cha and Destiny's first time here. They both was so amazed by the stores & scenery. Hey, let's go to Balenciaga first. "I had seen this Badd Ass Dress I like online.

Destiny: "Oh, we need details."

Tesla: The Balenciaga Dress is one sleeve body wrap for $1,650 and the Balenciaga Wrap-Around Heels for $695.00 to go with.

Cha-Cha: "Oh yeah that sound's real Badd."

Tesla: Cha-Cha it is!

Destiny: well, damn girl, I hate to see the price for the second date.

Tesla: "Just know Tesla is going to make a fashion statement where ever she goes.

"We can't wait to meet this Rayquan" Speaking of him, he is Face Timing me now!

Rayquan: "Good afternoon, beautiful; how is your day going?"

Tesla: It's going good. "How are you doing today?

Rayquan: "I'm good now. I'm talking to you."

Tesla: "You always seem to make me smile; hold on, I have two people I would like for you to meet. " Cha-Cha and Destiny come to the phone. "Rayquan, these are my two Best Friends. "This is Cha-Cha

Cha-Cha: "Hello, nice to meet you. I heard good things about you.

Rayquan: Hello Cha-Cha, nice to meet you as well

Tesla: "This is my other Best Friend Destiny

Destiny: Hello! "Damn, you are fine. "Yes!!! Best friend, keep him.

Rayquan: (Laughing) "Hello Destiny, nice to meet you.

Tesla: "Now that you have met my quiet and wild best friends, and they approve." I take it I have to see more of you.

Rayquan: "I wouldn't have any other way" "I will let you get back to hanging with your girls. See you tomorrow, enjoy your day, beautiful.

(Face Time Ended)

Chapter Seven
"OH SHIT 5-0 "

"That's odd. I didn't receive my morning text from Rayquan. "Maybe he is still sleeping. I guess I will text first today.

Tesla: Good morning, Handsome (8:00 A.M.)

"Glance at my phone still no text "hope he is ok."

Tesla: "I feel a vibration on my lap; this must be him

Rayquan: Good morning, Beautiful. "Sorry I'm late for texting, kind of overslept. I see you beat me to the punch. "I like that I was thought about. (11:00 A.M)

Tesla: "You are thought-about I was going to check on you. " You was off schedule this morning (just kidding) (11:02 AM)

Rayquan: "I will be on time tonight right now focus on the books, not me. "I can't have my girl failing. "I will be to pick you up at 7 o'clock. (11:05 AM)

"He so different any other guy wouldn't care nothing about my education. " I like this guy. He right; I'm daydreaming, and can't wait until I see him tonight. "School went by pretty fast today. Let me get home and shower and take a cap nap. "Rayquan will be at my house to pick me up at 7 o'clock. Let me set my alarm clock to wake me at 5:30 AM to wake me up. "Alarm clock going off" Let me go downstairs to the Beauty Bar and have Jada, do me some wand curls. Hey, Jada girl, can you do me some wand curls and my makeup? "I have a date tonight

Jada: A date?

Tesla: Yes, his name is Rayquan; he is so respectful, mature and makes me feel extraordinary.

Jada: "I can tell I see the glow."

Tesla: How was your day?

Jada: "It was great your mom and Cedes came down and got their hair done this morning. " I'm sorry what has gone on in your household. "How are you holding up?

Tesla: I have my moments, but no man should hit a female and especially not my mama. "He messed up our bond. I still love my dad, but he hurt me when he hurt my mama.

Jada: I'm praying for all of you "Ok, love you all set and looking fabulous as ever. Enjoy your date, be careful, and I can't wait to see and talk to you about it soon.

Tesla: Thank you, Jada. "I love it" let me go get change, we will talk soon; enjoy your evening.

Jada: "You as well, love."

Tesla: Let me get dress Rayquan will be on his way soon.

"Rayquan: "Let me go make this sale before I go pick up Tesla. Ok, everything good let me go ahead and pick up my girl. Ounce wave me down as I was about to pull off. "Aye Quan "can you drop me up to Smacks right quick? " Get in you need to make it quick I have somewhere to be. I pull up Smacks Ounce did what he had to do, heading back to drop Ounce off. "We smoking Ounce look in the side mirror. " Oh, shit, there goes 12" I see them but aye, chill, we almost back to your house. "I'm driving playing everything cool "Thank God my Driver's License & Registration Good. "I know we are riding dirty. I'm trying to get to Ounce House quickly as possible. "Soon as we got on 72nd only a block away from Ounce house. "Ounce jumped out of the car and started running. The Cops immediately turned on their siren and came to the car. The Officer said do you know why I pull you over? "I responded yes because my homeboy jumped out of the car, right? " He then started questioning me about why Ounce jump out. "I told him I only could answer for me; he asks for My License and Registration. " I gave it to him; he asks do I have any weapons in the car? "I said NO! He then asked me to step out of the vehicle to check the vehicle. "I knew I was going down, and this the wrong time. " Officer, please let me make an important call. " You can at the station he started reading me my rights and told me to watch my head as he put me in the back of the police car. " I wonder where Rayquan at its 7:15 PM he haven't called or text yet. "Let me take a couple of pictures and reply to Cha-Cha and Destiny Group Chat. " My girls are crazy let me call Rayquan. "I have called Rayquan four times and sent six text messages. " Still no response I know something wrong he wouldn't stand me up. He was looking forward to our date more than me. Mama and Cedes came to my room it was now 9 o'clock. Mama: Tesla, is everything ok?

Tesla: No, ma'am, I can't get in touch with Rayquan; this is not like him.

Mama: "Well, I pray he is ok as she kisses me on the cheek.

Cedes: "I do to sis"

Tesla: As tears ran down my face, it was for disappointment and Rayquan Safety that's all I could do is think about.

Rayquan: I'm sitting in the back seat like a damn kid. I could have just said No! But I thought about all the times I needed help, and people told me No! "I can't do nothing but own up to what I had in the car, and do my bid. " I got through the system with my finger prints, took my mud shot and answer all these intake questions. "Only thing on my mind is contacting Tesla. "Officer Pittman did let me get numbers out of my phone. He said I was the first person in that area that didn't give them a hard time. The only numbers I wanted out my phone were Tesla and My Lawyer. I'm calling Tesla, hoping she answer my phone call.

"Tesla: Cha-Cha, Let me call you back. I don't recognize this number; this might be Rayquan.

Chapter Eight
"You Have a Collect Call "

Hello! "You have a collect call from Rayquan; an Inmate at William's Road Jail. Do you accept the charges?

Tesla: Yes!

Rayquan: hey beautiful "I'm so sorry that I didn't make our date. I got to pull over after Ounce jump out of the car. "I understand if you never want to talk to me again.

Tesla: I am upset but happy you are ok and thought of me enough to call and apologize, and we are still cool; you owe me big time.

Rayquan: This means a lot to me; you showed me the different in a woman that all women are not the same.

Tesla: "You showed me different in a man.

Rayquan: Are you ok? "I know you were so beautiful tonight. I had a nice evening plan out; no worries, its set and stone when I get out.

Tesla: I'm better just can't wait to see you again. "At first, I thought you were my dad when I picked up and heard the recording. "I'm glad it was you. I'm not ready to talk to him yet.

Rayquan: Oh Wow! That's crazy we might run into each other. Oh there the queue. "We only get 15mins and have only 1 min remaining.

Unknown Inmate: Aye, hurry up. I got to use the phone.

Rayquan: "This clown behind me is acting stupid about the phone. He is going to wait his turn. "I want all 15mins shared with you. " I'm going to call you back in the morning; sweet dreams, beautiful.

Rayquan: Aye, I was on the phone with my girl. "Be early next time.

Unknown Inmate: "I own this youngster when I say I want to use the phone get off.

Rayquan: "I don't care what you run; it's just not me. My father dead and gone get out my way, man.

Unknown Inmate: Yeah, I see you around, youngster.

Tesla: "I laid back on the bed and felt so relieved that he was ok said my prayers, and turn on my Pandora.

Guards: Lights Out

Rayquan: staring at the ceiling. "Can't sleep just thinking about Tesla. "Dear God, remove me away from harm's way. Make me better, God, so I can stop selling drugs. "I finally found someone I want to be with. Make me a changed man in Jesus' name, amen. Man, let me get some rest and be the first one in line to use the phones to call Tesla and My Lawyer.

Diamond: "Good morning, how are you feeling this morning, baby?

Tesla: I'm feeling better. How are you mama?

Mama: "I'm doing just fine, baby. Did Rayquan ever call you and tell you why he didn't come?

Tesla: Yes, ma'am, he was arrested yesterday.

Mama:" OMG! "Baby, I hate that happen.

Tesla: "I was disappointed yesterday but happy that he reach out and going to make it up when he is released.

Mama: "Well, come downstairs to get a bite to eat.

Tesla: "Soon as mama left the room, I received an incoming call. "Hey, I recognize this number. "This Rayquan, I answer the call. "You have a collect call from an Inmate at William Road Jail. Do you accept the charges? Yes!

Rayquan:" Good morning, beautiful how did you sleep last night?

Tesla: good happy you're ok.

Rayquan: what are your plans for today?

Tesla: Going to the mall with Cha-Cha to get her daughter's ears pierced, maybe a little shopping and lunch.

Rayquan: well, that sounds nice. I want you to enjoy your day. "I just wanted to check on you. "Have a good day, beautiful!

Tesla: thank you, handsome, and try to make the best out of it in there. (Called Ended).

Rayquan: "Let's see what kind of breakfast they got in here. " Soon as I sat down here this big clown the one from the other day disrespecting me at the phone.

Unknown Inmate: Hey, I want to apologize to you youngster. "I took anger out on you. Just a lot of family shit I'm dealing with it. "My name

Broken In Broad Daylight

Dollar, what's yours?

Rayquan: apology, accepted my name Rayquan, and I know how that can be.

Dollar: what are you in here for?

Rayquan: Drug Charges, what about you?

Dollar: Domestic Violence and Alcohol waiting to see My Lawyer to get bond out. Shit! Touch my wife not accepting my calls and embarrassed even to call my daughters. I can't believe I beat their mother and let them see that abuse shows immaturity as a father.

Rayquan: Damn, I hate that happen to your family. As I shake my head and look at Dollar, this story sounds familiar. "I know this got to be Tesla Dad. I didn't ask her his name but it sounds like this could be him. Let me play it out as it goes.

Dollar: Got any kids yet?

Rayquan: No, maybe one day

Dollar: Take your time, but when you have one or two like myself, "it's the best feeling in the world.

Rayquan: What do you have, boy and girl? "See, I was trying to fit questions in on this conversation to see if this is Tesla Father.

Dollar: No two teenage girls, the love of my life.

Rayquan: "Yes, it's confirmed this him without having to say their names. I can tell by your response you love them.

Dollar: More than you ever know.

Rayquan: "They will come around; we all hurt differently the love you got for them they got for you. Try writing them "I know it helped me when I lost my parents at a young age and then my grandmother; the streets and the Cemetery are all I could turn to. "I use to go out to the Cemetery to read the letters I wrote to them and sit it there. "I was so angry at the truck driver that hit them, but it helped me cope with life. "I see the world differently now.

Dollar: Wow that's a lot sorry you went through that "that's a good idea. I will try that. Let's go out to the yard and lift weights.

Rayquan: "I was lifting 250 and Dollar lift 350 with one hand. I know his hands are made of steel. "Man, I'm standing here like damn that was fast wonder how Tesla would feel about this." Later that night, I called Tesla because I didn't want to keep anything from her if I wanted our relationship to work. "I ask Tesla what her dad's name was? "Said his real name Bernie but they call him Dollar. It was confirmed that Dollar is Tesla's Father. I let her know the other night when the guy rushing me off the phone was him. "She asked how I found out that was him? " He apologized for his behavior the other night at breakfast started talking about family concerns etc. "Tesla was shocked and wanted to keep it between us for now. " She didn't know how her dad's response will be and that she would let him know when he is released. The next couple of week's things were going well. My Lawyer was talking about me getting released soon. Tesla and I are doing well. "I'm hoping I get out in time for her Senior Prom and Graduation. The Guards had switched me upstairs to share a pod with Dollar. They saw how close we were. "Dollar and I talked, even more, that night about life. He asked me what I wanted to become. I told him to become A Barber and own my own barbershop. He asked me what's stopping me. "I said money, support, and a diploma. " He sat quiet with no response for a minute.

Dollar: have you thought about testing for your GED?

Rayquan: No

Dollar: Tomorrow we going down to library to study and then to The Salon so you can shadow The Barber cutting hair.

Rayquan: Thank you. I haven't had this type of support in a long time since I lost important people in my life, and ever since you came alone and my girl, my spirits have been lifted. "That new beginning do exist"

Dollar: I see a lot of potential in you, and I will support you. You have help me get back the relationship with my family and I have decided to put the drug life up. Enroll in AA and join a church. My children are getting older. My baby girl will be going to Prom in two weeks and graduating in 4weeks. I be damn! If I miss it. "It makes no sense to be in here and I can't be mad at anyone but myself and change it. " Everything I own is paid for and have money put up to continue to leave comfortable for my entire life. "I'm in here for unnecessary behavior. It makes no sense living in a square when I have a whole mansion, food, clothes, and shoes

Rayquan: "After weeks went by, I was finally was ready to take my GED this morning. " It's kind of a bittersweet day; today is the day I will accomplish my goal, and today Dollar will be released. He asked The Guards if he could be released after I took the test and they said he could since they haven't had any problems with him.

Examiner: "Good morning! " I'm your Examiner Mrs. Polite; you will have two hours to complete your test. Relax and good luck to everyone you may begin.

Rayquan: "I'm very nervous; my pencil kept slipping out of my hands. " Let me say a quick prayer before I start. "Prayer always help" Father God, "Thank you for this opportunity to learn new skills and stretch my understanding. Thank you for guiding me through this time of study into the final exams. I lay before you all the hopes and fears I have about the outcome. "In Jesus' name amen." The Examiner received my test and grading it. She told me I can continue my morning, and I will receive my results later. "Just received my test results from The Guard.

Dollar: What are you waiting for? "You won't know until you read it."

Rayquan: This letter is to inform you that you have passed the General

Educational Development (GED) at William County Jail as of May 25, 2021.

Dollar: So did you passed?

Rayquan: I looked at him for a minute like he did the first time we talked in our cell and said YES!!!

Dollar: My Boy, congratulations. I know you could do it.

Rayquan: Dollar hugged me with so much excitement.

Dollar: Next month, when you get out, go straight to Champions of Excellence Hair Academy. "Your Tuition is already paid for, and you got a New Bank Account at Faith Bank with $50,000 to start you off. "DON'T Let Me Down!!!

Rayquan: All I could do is cry and hug him tight. "I won't (repeatedly) "thank you so much."

Dollar: Guard, I'm ready to leave now my work here is done. "See you when I get out.

Rayquan: As the automatic doors were about to shut.

Dollar: what's your girlfriend's name again? I'm praying everything works out with the both of you?

Rayquan: Her name is Tesla

.

Chapter Nine
BREAKING NEWS

Guards: Take care, Mr. Oakwood Thanks for everything for making me see different about life in so little time. The next time you see me, will be at a Starbucks, and everything will be on me.

Guards: We hold you to it take the care.

Dollar: My Driver was picking me up felt different because I wished it was Diamond and the girls. "Again, Dollar, I'm responsible for all this, and I must make it right. I had my driver to pick up red steam roses for all three special ladies in my life. I can't wait to see my lovely ladies. "I arrived at the house; they had no idea I was coming home. Cedes answers the door.

Cedes: its daddy, y'all its daddy

Dollar: Cedes greeted me with a heartfelt hug and kiss. Tesla came running downstairs like she was the baby girl I remember her as.

Tesla: I missed you so much, and hug and kiss me.

Diamond: Welcome home, baby; welcome home & embrace me with a hug and kiss.

Dollar: Despite my wrongs, they made me still feel loved. "I'm so sorry, baby. I'm giving up all the street life, baby. I enrolled myself in AA I start Monday Morning I don't never want to be apart from my family again. How are my girls doing? We are good, daddy, happy you're home.

Tesla: Daddy, you made it home just in time for My Senior Prom. "Its next weekend. I'm so excited.

Dollar: I wouldn't miss it for anything in the world. "I'm very proud of the both of you." Let me go get clean up, and let's go out to dinner.

Diamond: Ok, baby, take your time we headed to the mall. "We will meet you at Ruth's, Chris.

Dollar: ok baby, see y'all shorty.

Tesla: we got in the car on the way to the mall mama immediately started making reservations for a party of 50, order a cake from Grama's Bakery, and having Cedes, and I call up all daddy's friends to be at the mall by 7 o'clock. "Everyone was not aware that daddy was coming home this was a big surprise for all of us, and we wanted daddy to feel welcome.

Mama: "Let's go in a couple of stores and buy him some new items. He is going to be very shocked by this.

Dollar: Hey Baby, I'm on my way now.

Diamond: ok baby, just tell the Host that you are looking for the Oakwood's when you get here.

Tesla: We arrived at Ruth's Chris with everything set up, mama had the stores to wrap daddy's welcome home gifts. All his friends came with no questions. The host already knew it was a surprise gathering for my dad and just to show daddy to the table when he arrives.

Ruth's Chris Host: Good evening, welcome to Ruth's Chris. How many people will be joining you today?

Dollar: Hello, I'm for the Oakwood's Party

Ruth's Chris Host: My apologies right this way, Sir! "Your party is already seated. SURPRISE!!!! Oh wow, I wasn't expecting this.

Tesla: Daddy quickly hugged mama and kept kissing her and came around the table hugging Cedes and I and was overwhelmed with joy from all his friends that came out.

Dollar: Man, I don't deserve this y'all do. I made wrong choices.

Diamond: We all love you, baby, and we're in this together; let's say a prayer eat and enjoy this time together.

Tesla: We laugh all evening, nothing but a good time.

Daddy's Friends: We out of here guys, everything was really nice we enjoyed every one of you welcome home Dollar we love you.

Dollar: Thanks again for coming out. I enjoy every one of you it was appreciated. "I enjoyed myself. " Tunk! " I'm going to head your way shortly if that's ok with you, baby?

Mama: "Yes, I'm ok with that, baby.

Dollar: ok, see you soon I'm going to talk to my girls first, and then I'll head your way.

Tunk: Ok Boss Man, see you soon.

Dollar: So how have you been, Cedes?

Cedes: "I been good just focus on School College is hard daddy.

Dollar: "Stay focused. You got this, and I'm always here for you for anything; remember that "I love you always" what about you Tesla? How have you been? I can't believe you got a month left and you are done with high school." Tesla: To be honest daddy, I was sad but happy now I met a friend when you were gone. "I know you don't want us to date, but he is different. I care about him, and he cares about me. "He makes sure I stay focused in school, God, and out of trouble. "I want the both of you to meet him soon when he is released from jail.

Dollar: No, dad wants to see their kids grow up. I can't make the decision for you, but I do approve of Rayquan. "Yeah, I met him in jail; he is a nice young man. I learn from him in jail to be a better father. He turned his life around in prison and I did too. I got to see this young man receive his GED, and I already enrolled him into Champions of Excellence Hair Academy when he is released paid in full Tuition and start him off with a good amount of money at Faith Bank.

Tesla: Are you serious, daddy? "I couldn't do nothing but come around and hug and kiss my daddy over and over again. " Here I go hiding this from him, and he knew all along. I'm so glad he got to know Rayquan in Jail. Dollar: I love all of you so much; remember Cedes and Tesla? "You both finish school and always take care of each other. No matter what comes around. You may not see eye to eye, but you are sisters; never let a man or friends come between the both of you.

Dollar: Baby, again, I apologize for putting my hands on you & disrespecting you, that will never happen again. "Love is not supposed to hurt.

Ruth's Chris Waiter: will anyone care for dessert?

Dollar: No thank you! We are all stuff, just the receipt, please.

Tesla: Daddy paid for everything, and it was his gathering. "We all got into the car daddy kiss us and told mama to drive safe he will be home soon.

As we were heading home, mama turn left daddy went right. "Mama noticed an intoxicated driver crossing over the light going Northbound on Kings Rd going in daddy direction.

Mama: Dear God, cover my husband and other drivers on Kings Rd and may they all bypassed this intoxicated driver. Amen. "Cedes, call 911 on your phone and put it on speaker so I can report this driver. 911: what's your emergency? "Hello, there, a Black F150 going down Kings Rd heading Northbound; the driver is intoxicated. Thank you. We will have someone look into this ASAP. "Cedes called your father, and Tesla call your Uncle Tunk and see if he made it there.

Cedes: "He not answering Mama.

Tesla: Uncle Tunk said no, daddy hasn't made it there yet mama.

Mama: That's odd. "I'm about to turn around; I feel something is wrong.

Tesla: As we headed down Kings Rd all you see are cars pieces and shattered glass all over the road. "Police lights flashing and Sirens as they appear to get closer. Mama jumped out of the car because they had the road blocked off. Call your father again.

Cedes: He still not answering.

Broken In Broad Daylight

Tesla: Mama started running up to the scene of the accident and going underneath the caution tape.

Officers: Ma'am, stand back; you can't come this way

Mama: No! "That's my husband. Somebody help him, please...

Tesla: Paramedics drag daddy and other drivers out there vehicles that were involved in this accident. The drunk driver and another driver died at the scene, and Daddy was the only person who survived and was transported to the hospital. Mama got in the ambulance with daddy and Cedes, and I drove behind them. "Daddy was still in ICU and still wasn't responsive. We all continue to pray for daddy very tiresome but wasn't giving up. Five days later, daddy regained consciousness mama was so happy and Cedes, and I was too. We kiss and hug daddy for hours. He just smiled he still wasn't talking yet. We headed downstairs to get some fresh air and bite to eat.

Mama: Thank you, God Dollar open his eyes, girls; it took some time, but we Oakwood's are Fighters.

Doctor Wells: "How about all of you go home and get some rest. Mr. Oakwood seems to be getting better, and it's essential that all of you get some rest.

Mama: I don't want to leave him.

Doctor Wells: He is in good hands. I will make sure I keep you updated, and welcomed to contact me anytime.

Tesla: "Later that night we went home we said our love you and kiss daddy good night. We got our hot shower, and rest felt relief that daddy was doing better. Doctor Wells call mama at 10:18 AM and informed us that daddy had a Brain Aneurysm and that they did all they could do and give us their deepest condolences. Mama dropped her phone and cry so hard in the middle of the floor. Cedes, and I was emotional was a wreck but was thankful that we had got to share our final moments with him.

Chapter Ten
"I'LL BE MISSING YOU "

"That evening mama called around to daddy's friends and told them that daddy had passed away. They all took it very hard and were on the first flight to be with us and help mama with funeral arrangements. "I contacted William Road Jail and asked could a priest informed Rayquan that my dad had passed away. Rayquan sent his condolences to us. "He cried so hard on the phone. "Saying he was so sorry this happened and wished he could be with me in my time of need. "Cha-Cha and Destiny have called me every day true definition of best friends. The next day, most of our family & friends had landed in from all over to pay their respects to daddy. "Over 7 Hotels were completely book for my daddy's funeral alone. Mama had a farewell gathering with seafood and liquor just enjoy each other company, and daddy wouldn't want us to mourn. Mama and Daddy's Friends were making sure they lay daddy to rest the correct way. "They got daddy, limousines, horse and carriage, doves, red carpet, flowers. Daddy always wanted his funeral at a southern church to have his funeral like Mama P. "The same day we have daddy's funeral is the same day as my senior prom." I had no desire to go anymore after daddy passed and Rayquan was still in jail. So I ask could daddy colors be black and silver like my prom dress and accessories and walk in with red roses. Mama love that idea and was unfortunate that this happened at the end of my senior year and how much daddy was looking forward of me graduating and prom night. I let mama know that daddy will still see me walk across the stage in sprint and that I will play the piano as we use to at his funeral. "DANCE WITH MY FATHER". Mama: aww, we have raised such a mature young lady. "Tesla, this is so sweet of you. "Most children of your age would have been complaining and crying about prom. "You haven't been selfish and this has lifted my sprints. I was so depressed inside and to know I can lean on my children for support means the world to me.

Tesla: Mama, my heart is broken that daddy will never be back. "I cry in my room, look at pictures, and replay our funny videos and our favorite songs, but I know he would want us all to stay strong. " He always use to tell us if anything happens to him, you take care of us, and Cedes look after me. We are Oakwood's stick together no matter what. "This moment will never go unnoticed" I'm incredibly proud of both of you; I can't express it enough. How about Cedes and I wear black gowns and ask everyone else to wear red and sliver?

Tesla: "I like how that sounds, mama.

Cedes: "Hey, Mama and Tesla do you like this crown for daddy? Mama: I love it, Cedes, it's beautiful. We went down to the "PRATER'S FUNERAL HOME" to finalize all daddy funeral arrangements and to view daddy's body for the first time. Daddy's Friends out did themselves daddy had a Clear Casket with a Giorgio Armani Suit with Christian Louboutin Alpha Male on with a Red Rose Corsage on his suit daddy look so good. "Mama didn't want to view daddy as how she pictures him in the hospital. "She wanted to view daddy if he was sleeping peacefully, and Prater's Funeral Home and Daddy's Friends met our expectations. Daddy looked so handsome. We talk to daddy, laugh, and cry simultaneously, reminiscing on all the good memories. This was our time alone that one last time. Mama didn't want us to go to wake; she said we been through enough and need to go home and rest and prepare for tomorrow. The following day we got up and started to get dress and prepare for daddy's funeral. No one had an appetite, but the family wanted us to eat something. When we came downstairs, our house had so many beautiful flowers from all over, even William Road Jail and Rayquan had flower arrangements delivered. We walk around the living room and read how Daddy had a significant impact on many people's lives that we knew nothing about. Daddy had banners, catered food with caters for daddy repast a live band. When we got dressed and headed out to Amazing Grace Church of God & Christ, the funeral will be held. As we turn out our gates, cars were honking. People had pictures on their shirts, pants, shoes, even their vehicles of daddy. Our family lined up to come in the churches we began to enter the church. "The AGC Choir song "I SHALL WEAR A CROWN." People were in the church saying how beautiful we were as we walk in. The Choir continue singing until my entire family was seated. The Funeral Director came in and crowned daddy. It was simply beautiful, Cedes gave a Tribute to Honor Daddy. "Auntie Bridgette mime danced to "TAKE ME TO THE KING"; Uncle Tunk, Auntie Shenell & Cousin Brett gave words of Reflections. " Uncle Tunk took it really hard because daddy was supposed to come to his house after dinner but never made it. "He told the audience of the funeral how that will forever replay in his head the last time he talk to his best friend. " I played "DANCE WITH MY FATHER" on the piano and express how I was feeling as I played each note without singing. Bishop Wright preached the word of Forgiveness. Daddy Pallbearers were his Best Friends Robert, Brett, Leon, Earl, Otis, and Bernard. With three on both sides, they lift daddy as they begin to walk daddy out of the church. "The AGC Choir began singing "FOREVER by Jason Nelson." I put on my all black diamond visor shades on because my eyes was so puffy from crying. My legs began to shake as I began to walk down the aisle. I started to feel weak. I felt like I lost my best friend but gained an angel at the same time. I exit the doors of the church into daylight. Starring at the casket "I'm Broken In Broad Daylight

Book Cast Members
Bernie A.K.A Dollar (The Daddy)
Mama P (Tesla Deceased Grandmother)
Diamond (Mother)
Mercedes (Sister)
Tesla (Daughter & Main Character)
Destiny & Chasity A.K.A. Cha-Cha (Tesla Best Friends)
Star (Cha-Cha Daughter)
Lil Zack (Destiny Brother)
Big Mama (Destiny Grandmother)
Lonnie (Guy on D-Block)
Jahiem (Cedes Deceased Boyfriend)
Rayquan (Tesla Boyfriend)
Hattie Mae (Rayquan Deceased Grandmother)
Ounce (Rayquan Homeboy)
Monica & Courtney (Neighbors)
Mahan (Store Owner)
Mr. Wells (Doctor)
Donald (Ruth's Chris Waiter)
Tracy (Flight Attendant)
Jada (Beautician)
Tunk, Leon, Robert, Brett, Otis & Bernard (Dollar Best Friends)
Auntie Bridgette, Shenell & Cousin Brett (Family Members in Funeral)
Mr. Donell (Tesla History Teacher)
Ms. Smith (Gossip Staff at Tesla School)
Ms. Hart (Tesla Math Teacher)
Mr. Troy (Tesla Home Room Teacher)
Mr. Ross (Tesla Principal)
Officer Pittman (At Williams Road Jail)
Mrs. Polite (GED Examiner)

www.ingramcontent.com/pod-product-compliance
Lightning Source LLC
Chambersburg PA
CBHW061505170626
46811CB00004B/1610